Darling Baby

Maira Kalman

Little, Brown and Company
New York Boston

البتة

Today we watched
a SEAGULL
fly overhead.
He was carrying
a SILVER Fish
in his CLAWS.
The SEAGULL had a
pointy YELLOW beak and
PINK LEGS.
The fish had an angry LOOK.

At Night
there WAS A
FIERCE STORM.
Lightning and Thunder
filled the DARK SKY.
LATER the STARS came out.
But we were
ASLeep.

For the invincible and inspiring Olive and Esme and
for the ones to come.

With great thanks to
Charlotte Sheedy, Susan Rich, Saho Fujii
for the seasons to come.

ABOUT THIS BOOK: The illustrations for this book were done in gouache on Fabriano Artistico 140 lb. hot press paper. This book was edited by Susan Rich and designed by Saho Fujii. The production was supervised by Ruiko Tokunaga, and the production editor was Jen Graham. The text was hand-lettered.

First Edition: June 2021 • Little, Brown and Company is a division of Hachette Book Group, Inc. • The Little, Brown name and logo are trademarks of Hachette Book Group, Inc. • The publisher is not responsible for websites (or their content) that are not owned by the publisher. • Library of Congress Cataloging-in-Publication Data • Names: Kalman, Maira, author. • Title: Darling baby / Maira Kalman. Description: First edition. | New York : Little, Brown and Company, 2021. | Audience: Ages 4–8. | Summary: "Based on the journal she kept when her granddaughter was new, Maira Kalman shares observations about a summer spent with a baby." —Provided by publisher. Identifiers: LCCN 2020018312 (print) | ISBN 9780316330626 (hardcover) • Subjects: CYAC: Babies—Fiction. | Grandparent and child—Fiction. | Nature—Fiction. • Classification: LCC PZ7.K1256 Dar 2021 (print) | DDC [E]—dc23 • LC record available at https://lccn.loc.gov/2020018312 • ISBN: 978-0-316-33062-6 • PRINTED IN CHINA • APS • 10 9 8 7 6 5 4 3 2 1

Today
a thousand tiny
silver fish jumped out
of the water at the
SAME Time. They arced OVER
the water and quickly dove in again,
disappearing in the wet green SEA.

Today we found

a Black Stone

a Pink shell

a white stone.

A man in a RED Shirt glided by.
A BLACK DOG was his companion.

I wanted to yell out and ask the
man what his dog's name was.
But I didn't. Maybe I felt SHY.
OR I didn't want to disturb the QUIET.
IF the SILVER Fish were jumping today,
we did not see them because we went to a PARTY.

It was SUMMER and Fine.

We celebrated your birth and EVERYONE'S BIRTHday with cheery CHeRRy PIE.

We went outside and saw
a TREE filled with yellow sparkly STARS.

OH.

I forgot to
TELL you.
At the party, a
man liked the
CHEERY
CHERRY
PIE.
"TAKE it HOME",
said a woman.
"HOW
will I take it home?"
He thought
and said,
"I WILL put it in
my HAT."
And he DID.

We took a NAP on the LAWN. WHILE WE SLEPT, 3 BLACK BiRDS LOOKED FOR WORMS to EAT. A mother RABBiT and her BABY RABBiT Ran By. Now and Then they stopped to munch on some FRESH gREEN GRASS. But they did NOT turn GREEN.

You had to go away for a few DAYS.
I LOOKed at the waTeR without you.

The Fish.
  The BiRDS.
    The Bunnies.
   The SuN. The sTaRS.
ALL of these things
      STAYed.
It was fine to
    see them
    Without You.
      But not the SAME.

Something else happened.

I saw a
Big Mossy-Green Turtle on
the BEACH. I was so excited.
But then I noticed he was not moving.
At ALL. And then I saw that he was
NO LONGER ALIVE.
One minute I was so happy.
The next, so sad.
The water carried the tURtLE
out to SEA to be buRied in the
VAST ocean. I think thAt is a
Good Thing. At any Rate, it is a thing.
I am telling you this because I
know you will understand.

Today you came back. HURRAH! We went to a diner for BREAKFAST. A man wearing a Red hat, Red shirt, and Red shorts was eating blueberry pancakes. A woman leaned her head to one SIDE.

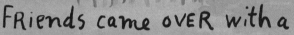

FRiends came OVER with a BIG RED BALL. OSKAR the DOG Looked unhappy in his sweater.

Today we saw a
HOLE in the GRASS.

Do you know how it got there?

The Bunny dug it. I am
PRETTY SURE because bunnies
Live in
HOLES
in the GROUND.

We woke up EARLY
and saw 31 Geese
Gliding on the WATER.

Silently,
Slowly, they
moved together.

The MOON came OUT and it was FULL.

WE LiT SPaRKLeRS to CeLeBRaTe more BiRThdAYS. EVeryone is BORN. That is TRUE.

Dancers came to visit.

We
watched them
DANCE.
The BIRD.
The BUNNY.
You
and
I.

The GEESE swam by again.
But this time there were only 29.
Where did the other two go?

By the way,
ducks, literally,
QUACK.

We met a CURLY dog named Belle.

She was in LOVE with a DOG named

Ferdinand.
He had two brown dots over his eyes.
Almost like an extra pair of eyes.

The water was pink
this morning.
You were sleeping.

The water has Been
BLUE and GReen and
GRAY and BLACK
and PINK.

Darling Baby,
When you
wake up from
Your NAP,
we will
GO
for a WALK.

I will CARRY you because you can't WALK yet. We will LOOK at the Blue Sea, Red Flowers, Green Grass. I will say, "LOOK at this, LOOK at that." You won't answer because you can't speak yet. But you will LOOK at EVERYthing. And EVERything is Really Quite BEAUTIFUL. Quite.